Roller Madonnas

Bernard Ashley

Illustrated by Kim Harley

A & C Black · London

Roller Madonnas

GRAFFIX

First paperback edition 1997
Reprinted 1998

First published in hardback by A & C Black (Publishers) Ltd
35 Bedford Row, London WC1R 4JH

Text copyright © 1997 Bernard Ashley
Illustrations copyright © 1997 Kim Harley

ISBN 0-7136-4708-6

A CIP catalogue record for this book is available from
the British Library.

Printed in Great Britain by William Clowes Ltd,
Beccles, Suffolk

Thank God It's Friday

Going home from school was so slow. Walking. It was like you had a rope round you, pulling you back, or as if someone were holding a magnet to your backside.

The two slouched on, lugging Adidas bags of homework, moaning on - but only for the sake of it, because it was Friday. Friday! The end of the school week - when Saturday meant Pelham Park and two miles of baby smooth tarmac for roller blading. And the pair of them would be there, gliding and sliding - cool helmets, Skate Smart kneepads, carving the arc in identical gear: Maria and Mary, the two Madonnas on blades.

Maria Charles and Mary Webster. Year Seven.
One black and full of figure, the other white
and slim enough for the cat walk.
And both as flash as lightning.

Mary had come to her corner. They did a one-handed high five, and she went off with her nose already twitching at the thought of fish and chips.

Maria ran on a couple more turnings to the street in the sky which was Mandela House.

As usual, the lift had the 'out of order' sign up: but what were two landings when you were thirteen, and fit as a Gladiator?

out of order

She ran up the stairs, fished for her key, and bounced inside for the start of the weekend. Friday!

9

Rainy Days

Something stopped Maria throwing her bag on the floor. Her dad didn't like her doing that - and what was that on the coat pegs? Not just the empty wall hanging there, but his Railtrack jacket. He was home from his shift - but he was on two to ten this week. He shouldn't be in the flat.

Maria put down her bag like it was filled with eggs and walked quietly into the living room. Dad was sitting in his armchair looking like a man expecting the Reverend to call, like a man who didn't belong in his own home. Through in the kitchen her mam was making tea; milk, sugar, and a nip of something naughty.

Come in, girl, I ain't a ghost.

But he looked like one. His face had on it that grey tinge tarmac has. And for a big man he had a shrink to him, sitting there.

His eyes looked into hers, refused to blink, but they were wet.

Wassup, Dad? They sent you home ill?

They sent him home sacked. They sent him home re-dun-dant!

Maria's mam came in from the kitchen, spelling-out the verdict the way she would have called it out in church.

Maria wanted to run over and hug him, but the big man looked as if he might break into bits.
Why? An' why you?
It's his level going, the ones with all the 'up here'.
They're keeping the sweat an' pickaxes, but they're changing him for a computer terminal.

Now Maria did risk his health. She went to his lap, and hugged her arms round his neck.

Starry Eyes

All the same, ten o'clock on the Saturday and Pelham Park was still the place to be, over the youth side. No grit put down in the zone signed up for skating, but a silky smooth tarmac to help when you went on your bum. And there were all the concrete curves and iron rails for the specialist stuff - 'getting air' by jumping, and 'grinding' along the rail like someone skating on a tightrope.

Coming up to the park took Maria out of herself. Home had suddenly got a sad edge to it, as if you had to park your smiles at the entrance. Everyone went about their business with a manner which said that making toast or coffee was career stuff.

And her father's face had taken on a real rusted bearings look to it. But up here she could forget it all for a bit - then go back home with a bit of breeze behind her.

17

And talking about trying to put a smile on someone's face - what was Mary doing, losing her balance and going down on her knees?

Who was she looking across at? Who was that new boy on the patch, grinding the rail?

He was good. He'd got all the gear. Ultra wheels, Slick knee and wrist guards, and a Cool-lid helmet. And he was tall and black and beautiful.

Crazy!

Maria went into a skid herself; feeling as smart as a toddler on the ice.

19

The boy came off the rail and went for the 'half pipe', shot up the concrete curve in a big way, and came back to stop dead with a power slide.
And as he glided off to take the downhill to the gates, they saw what was written on his back.

Monday, Monday

People looking for work start off like footballers
running out for a game. A clean kit, a glint in the
eye, and head held hope high. Maria caught herself
between a choke and a cry when she saw her dad
ready to start out on the Monday morning. He was in
his weddings and funerals suit, and he checked
himself in the mirror like a boy going off to a new
school. His smile was trembly, and so was his voice.

Maria's mam thought he meant what he said - that was his style.

You look *fit for* startin' at the top, but you take what they've got goin'...

Answering back stopped her mam from crying - but seeing him walk out on to the landing like he was off to run Marks and Spencers had her hand shaking the door shut with a bang she couldn't help.

Before setting out for school, Maria waited until she was sure she wouldn't bump into him at the bus stop.

It would have been a down day: Monday for a start, her poor old dad for seconds. But things looked up when she got to school. She and Mary hadn't been slouched in the tutor room two minutes, when in came Bad Breath Johnston with someone new. It was the boy with the serious blades. Danny Someone.

Maria nudged Mary, who had her head on her bag and her eyes closed.

Do what?

Maria said it all with her eyes.

And Mary sat up like a circus seal for the fish.

It was the snap inspection every new kid took. During the day he'd be sounded out on football teams and music. But you could tell from this first entrance, no one was going to take any liberties. He was his own man, this Danny Someone.

The name's Annand,
Daniel Leroy. Come
from Tulse Hill.

He looked round the room daring anyone to pick any
bones out of that.

Maria held herself off
from giving him a little
wave. He wouldn't have
seen her the way she'd
seen him on Saturday.
He was the one doing
the extreme roller
blading, not her.

Danny Annand was
nodding down the room
at Micky Fish. That figured.
Micky was a roller blader
like them, and quite good.

So Danny Annand found his place, next to Micky
Fish. And the two Madonnas kept their faces
straight, just smiled a bit inside.

Whoa!

Monday night was light on homework. Reading for English, corrections for Maths, and "be good to your people" for Religious Education. For the two Madonnas, the real up side was it gave them time for another skate in Pelham Park.

It was in-the-flat-and-out for Maria.

The first day hadn't gone so good for her dad, and it looked like he wasn't going to be running Marks and Spencers just yet. He spent a long time in the bedroom, folding and refolding his job-seek trousers over the chair. No doubt about it, the tarmac at the park was the place to be, and the spring evening would give them a good hour and a half of light.

Surprise - Mary was already up there when Maria buzzed in through the gates. This was a first, because Mary had duties with her little brothers before she could ever come out. But, no surprise - because who was there?

Only Micky Fish and Danny the Man.

It looked like Mary and the boys weren't having anything to do with one another, and Maria kept it that way.

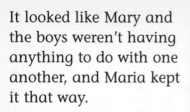

She'd come for the glide, hadn't she? Danny and Micky were taking turns at jumping over a bench.

The two Madonnas stuck to putting on speed and then emergency braking with hockey stops. But without so much as a twist of their necks they saw everything the others were doing.

First contact came by accident. And what a bump!
Danny the Man had come over the bench with a bus
to spare, landed, and had to put in a step to head off
a collapse.

Maria had had a stop
go wrong and shot on
like a sleep walker on
ice. On collision course.

She buffered into Danny and they spun in his clutch - a privilege he held on to well after their balance was back.

He let go, and she reverse vee'd to put some space in. He was smiling, but not lairy. She stuck herself out, made the best of everything for a second or so, and then rolled back to Mary, who was resting on a bench.

Maria sat down and looked at a wheel which didn't need looking at.

34

Maria didn't like coming second in anything. She looked back over at Danny, who was skating off with Micky Fish. She looked at the straight up and down of the other Madonna.

He said I was padded up a treat.

Mary nodded, the slightest of sniffs and got up.

Bit of a drawback, mind. Lucky you - got less wind resistance, with your figure.

But the smug look on her face said how jealous she was of that!

The Old Crew

When Maria got in from the park, there was a wet dab to the eyes going on again. Not the angry tears of the Friday before, but the warm weep of someone saying something nice. Charlie Cutler had called - the Railtrack supervisor from her dad's depot.

Dad was so straightfaced he could have been
kneeling before the Queen. But his voice broke
away from him like oiled wheels on the wet.

Maria hugged and kissed him so hard and strong it would keep him into his old age.

Maria's mam pulled out the yellow pages from under the sofa.

Maria put in a little skip as she went to her bedroom. Homework. She settled on her bed, opened the book, a bit of Judy Blume.

But, one way or another, Judy Blume wouldn't go in. Not even Judy Blume - because Maria's mind was blocked to bursting, her face fighting the smile off. And, to be honest, the smile was nothing to do with being pleased for her dad, but with the gliding into Danny Annand. The collision, the being close, him holding her a bit longer than he had to. Better even than gold watches, collisions like that...

Sweet and Sour

There weren't many days when getting to school was the number one thing to do. But Maria's Tuesday wake-up was with wide-awake eyes and quick feet to the floor. She gave the bathroom mirror a polish and checked herself out for zits and out-of-line eyebrows.

She combed her hair
and found a ribbon
the colour of the name
on Danny's back.
She wore Wednesday's
school sweatshirt
a day in advance,
and showed her shoes
the shining brush.

And as her dad went
out with a blunted crease
in his trousers, she waved
him off in a skirt sharp
enough to cut ice.

43

They were waiting for her in the school yard. Mary, Micky Fish and Danny. Mary sitting on a bench, Danny with a foot up like a captain giving a team-talk, and Micky Fish on the look-out for Maria. Maria walked over to them, trying to put some glide into her step.

These guys were telling me you call yourselves the Two Madonnas.

Uh-huh.

Danny was smiling a bit superior, but Maria let him off with it.

In her head, Maria pushed off for a backwards crossover, right round the bench to resume her cool stand.

Maria was glad she wasn't on rollers. She'd have collapsed, on her bum. Danny the Man asking her out with Mary and Micky Fish. It was just the sort of story running through her head which had blocked Judy Blume last night.

'I'm on,' she said, in a voice coming out like Minny Mouse. 'Sure.'

Danny winked at Mary and gave Micky the thumbs up.

The bell sounded for registration and they headed inside. 'When is it?' Maria asked, close enough to Danny to touch arms going in.

She went in happy - till halfway up the first staircase when it hit her. She was double booked. Saturday night was her dad's gold watch celebration. When these three were in their cinema seats, she'd be in the back of a minibus, halfway round the South Circular.

The Edge of the Blade

What a smack in the face! Maria's jaw went tight with trying not to show it. A diamond of a night out with Danny the Man, against being with her dad's old mates and the Peckham aunties. And she knew where she had to be. There wasn't any lucky dip about this. She had to be with her dad on his big night.

But Danny had four tickets, and he wasn't going to waste one, was he?

Maria said nothing until break, when she got hold of Mary in the girls' toilets.

They stood and stared at each other, until,

I bet your dad would've gone with us. I bet he was a sparky ol' pup.

And he's had his youth, he knows that. He's not gonna stop you having yours.

He expects me there.

He expects, but he doesn't demand. It's a pension do, it's for the old 'uns.

You'll be sitting on a chair with a flat lemonade listening to all the 'olden days' tales. It's gonna be down memory lane, all night...

51

Maria warmed up a bit at the thought -
to around gas mark five.

Gas mark ten.

Easy Peasy

Maria felt electric! She couldn't believe it had gone so well. She'd had a good think, and she'd come out with her lie as smooth as the ironing she was doing.

And they took Mary's story like it was God's truth. They said what a shame - of course - and left it at that, just made the usual noises about who'd bring her home and at what time? They knew Mary, liked her, she acted like the real Madonna when she came round. So that was it! The night out with Danny the Man was on again.

Perhaps it was true, what Mary had said. Perhaps her dad did see his celebration as more of a grown-ups' thing. And he had had his life, this was it here with her mam - while hers was still round the corner waiting for the chance to get started. And a night at the cinema with Danny the Man could be just the start it needed.

The other Madonna punched air at the news.

What do you reckon we ought to wear

Maria looked her up and down.

But she knew. Something which showed a bit
of shoulder, and not too loose - in fact, skin tight.
If you've got it, flaunt it! And she'd got a great
new skirt, with the white socks and black trainers.
She was really going to light up the dark in the
Coronet on Saturday.

The night out was the talk of the tutor room. People had her married off to Danny Annand.

Don't-do-anything-I-wouldn't do.

Micky Fish and Mary they were quieter about.
Well, they were a quieter pair all round.
And all the skating jokes.

Make sure you keep your bearings.

Hope you're in line for a good time.

No rollering down the aisles.

Maria smiled at Danny and took it coolly. He looked
as if he hadn't heard. Till he told her quietly,

The two Madonnas walked home, in silence. There
was too much going on inside their heads for talk.

Ready, Steady...

By the time Saturday afternoon
came, Maria didn't know *how* she
felt. On the one hand it was
like being on the top floor
balcony on a windy
day - hard to breathe,
and a bit light in
the head. And like
going down the first
drop on Death Ride
at Blackpool, guts
changing places
with your hair style.
That was the going
out with Danny.
And on the other,
it was like blading
on to oil and losing
it at speed, getting
grazed. That was
the letting down
of her dad.

She felt like a pair of scale pans - and which pan was up and which pan was down depended on whether she was in her own room at the mirror, or in the main room with her folks watching the clock on the wall.

What she wore had to be given careful thought. She couldn't knock any eyes out if she was supposed to be going to Mary's. So she went for a sporty look, the electric sweatshirt and bum tight jeans. The lipstick and eye stuff would have to wait for a shop doorway.

And at last the time came.
She double checked.

She closed her eyes and
dipped into that carton
of popcorn she and Danny
would be sharing - before
he held her hand, or put
his arm round her.

Inside herself, she screamed
down that Death Ride, but
on the outside she put on a
sad face for looking normal
in the living room.

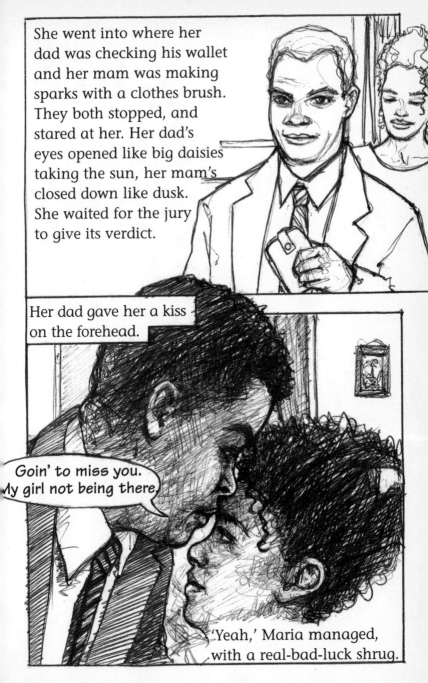

She went into where her dad was checking his wallet and her mam was making sparks with a clothes brush. They both stopped, and stared at her. Her dad's eyes opened like big daisies taking the sun, her mam's closed down like dusk. She waited for the jury to give its verdict.

Her dad gave her a kiss on the forehead.

Goin' to miss you. My girl not being there.

'Yeah,' Maria managed, with a real-bad-luck shrug.

It sure is a pity.
I could have got a minibus
the one size smaller...

Inside, Maria suddenly
wanted to cry. But she held
on, enough to call out from
the doorway,

Good luck, Dad.
Have a great time...

Which got her out - to run
to the first closed shop to
put on her make-up, and
start thinking forwards,
not back there.

Go!

There were five screens at the Coronet, of which Maria's Screen One was the best choice - no argument. "City In-line", total adrenalin. But the film wasn't the reason. She could have been heading for Screen Three - "All's Well that Ends Well" - and still felt just as good. It was because of who was standing over there, with the other two; Danny the Man.

She hurried over to the queue for Screen One. The backward baseball caps and the dude slicks, the floppy tops and the lycra, all going on about spins and grapevines and barrel rolls and stair riding. But Maria was looking for more personal talk.

She and Mary rubbed their heads, Mary not touching her hair, it was done too pretty. So was her slinky black top.

Danny had gone quiet, searching out his tickets as if he'd won four but lost one. As if someone was in for a smack into a lamp post. Maria stood a bit close to him. It wasn't going to be her missing out. But at last he found the fourth ticket, and they pressed on into Screen One.

It was filling up inside. And it was dark. An usher took them down the aisle with his torch. Centre seats, half way back.

They came to their row. The curtains were doing their crinkled curtsey down and up as they edged in past the knees. Danny, Mary, Maria and Micky. In that order.

In that order? They'd gone in wrong! Maria wanted to stop. She'd thought Mary would hold back for her to go in after Danny, but she hadn't. Well, she'd have to do it at the seats, leave the space for Maria to go on past.

But she didn't. Mary went along and sat down next to Danny the Man.

Maria sat. Just the one film, no interval. No getting up and changing any places after this. It had all gone wrong!

And no word from Danny. She looked along the row, but he was staring up at the screen while the sounds of traffic and the buzz of bearings started racing around for the titles.

"City In-line". Thump, thump, thump, and a wailing guitar swept them along a grey city street. Extreme speed roller blading. Cars swerved around and litter-bins jumped. A steep set of subway stairs were ridden - backwards, with a hockey stop at the bottom before someone went under a train.

A draw-in of breath, the whole cinema. And, to Maria's right, the eye catch of a hand coming round Mary's shoulder. Danny's hand - reaching to tap her?

It was not. It was squeezing Mary in tight to him, and Mary was going, with a little noise. Micky Fish pushed his popcorn tub on to Maria's lap.

He parked the tub between his legs and felt over again on to Maria's lap, staring at the screen as if his hand was on automatic. It found hers.

Get off!

She tried to put her hand somewhere out of the way. He had another grope, touched the top of her leg instead by accident, and giggled. But that was it for Maria.

Come on, Mair.

Gotta go to the lav.

Mary didn't seem
to be hearing.

Maria pushed past Micky,
knocking his popcorn over,
and rushed to the back of
the cinema, out of Screen
One and into the Ladies.

Blade Runner

She slammed into a cubicle and sat, stood, sat,
flushed the cistern, sat again. And stood.

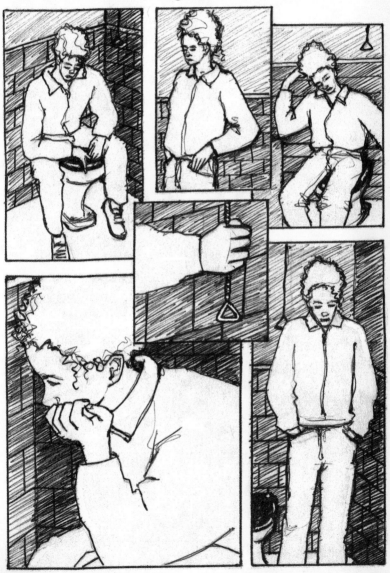

What a slap in the face!
Danny Annand and Mary

He'd got the wrong
Madonna in the
biggest way! So, what
sort of friend had
Mary been, not to let
on during the week?
She'd known! She was
always already there
with him, wasn't she?
They'd got their act
well sorted out, the
three of them. Mary
knew who was with
who long before they'd
gone down that aisle
like mixed-up brides.

What a show up! What a waste of time! And then it hit her like a hockey stick in the belly. The being here instead of in that minibus with her dear old dad, going on his celebration - the man she'd stood up for this!

Selfish little madam- coming here instead of being where I should have been!

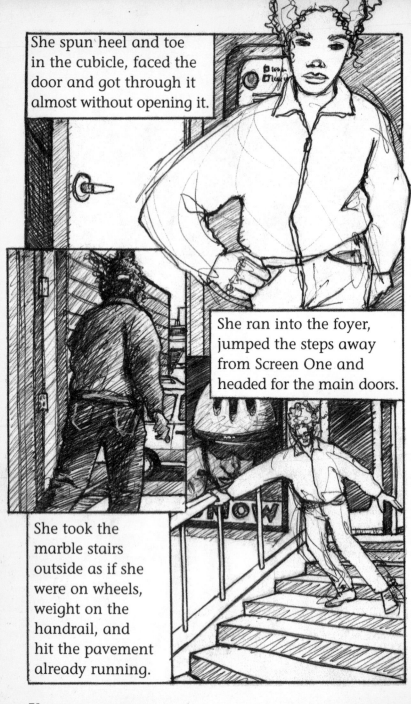

She spun heel and toe in the cubicle, faced the door and got through it almost without opening it.

She ran into the foyer, jumped the steps away from Screen One and headed for the main doors.

She took the marble stairs outside as if she were on wheels, weight on the handrail, and hit the pavement already running.

Seven o'clock, just after! The minibus was pulling away at quarter past.

On her wheels she'd have made it, no problem. But on her feet she wouldn't: not unless there was a delay at the flats, a lost hat or handbag. Or unless she forgot all the slide and glide of roller blading and went for it like an Olympic runner. Running for Britain. Running for her family. Running for her dad. Her true, trusted, loving, one-hundred-per-cent dad.

She put her head down and lifted her knees like a hundred metres' sprinter. She forced power into her stride. Because she *was* going to make it. Make it or die. The speed Madonna was going to be there, on her own two feet.

Just see her burn, all you blades!